Stories from
Mudpuddle Farm

Michael Morpurgo and Shoo Rayner

A & C Black · London

Contents

First published in one hardback
volume 1995 by
A & C Black (Publishers) Ltd
35 Bedford Row, London WC1R 4JH

And Pigs Might Fly!; Martians at
Mudpuddle Farm; Jigger's Day Off
first published by
A & C Black (Publishers) Limited
1990, 1991, 1992

Text copyright © Michael Morpurgo
1990, 1991, 1992, 1995
Illustrations © Shoo Rayner 1990,
1991, 1992, 1995

ISBN 0–7136–4267–X

Printed and bound in Great Britain by
Hunter and Foulis Ltd, Edinburgh

And Pigs Might Fly!

Chapter One

There was once a family of all sorts of animals that lived in the farmyard behind the tumble down barn on Mudpuddle Farm.

At first light every morning Frederick, the flame-feathered cockerel, lifted his eyes to the sun and crowed and crowed until the light came on in old Farmer Rafferty's bedroom window.

Ah sweet mystery of light, at last I've found you.

One by one the animals crept out into the dawn and stretched and yawned and scratched themselves. But no one ever spoke a word—not until after breakfast.

Old Farmer Rafferty put in his teeth, looked out of his bathroom window and shook his head.

And he opened the window and shouted,

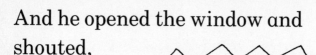

But the sun was too far away to hear. It just went on shining.

Chapter Two

Out in the farmyard the animals looked up at the sun and sighed.

So they all put their hats on, except for Egbert the greedy goat who had already eaten his –

and Pintsize
who thought pigs looked silly in
hats. But then Pintsize *never* did
what he was told.

9

Down at the pond Upside and Down, the two white ducks that no one could tell apart, had their heads stuck in the mud because there was hardly any water left in the pond.

Albertine sat still as a statue on her island, shading her goslings under her great white wings.

10

'When's it going to rain, Mum?'
they peeped.

'Sometime,' she said, and she
settled down to sleep because it was
the wisest thing to do and Albertine
was the wisest goose that ever lived
(and everyone knew it, including
Albertine).

So, thirsty and dusty and itchy, the animals trooped down to ask her advice, all except Mossop, the cat with the one and single eye, who was fast asleep on his tractor seat.

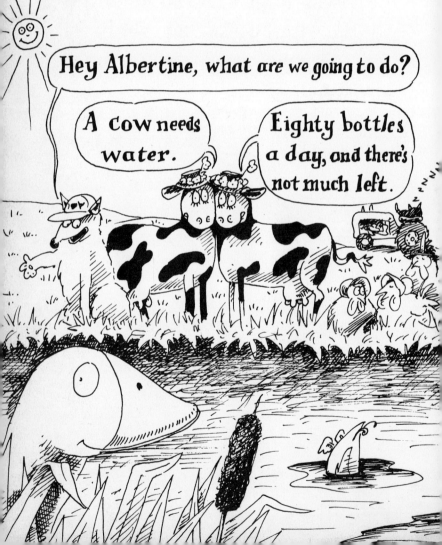

'What about you?' said Jigger, the almost-always sensible sheepdog.

Frederick looked up at the buzzards
and larks and swifts and swallows.
'If only I could fly like them. Must
be cool up there,' he sighed.

And little Pintsize looked up too
and thought just the same thing.

15

'You've got wings,' said Egbert.
'Use them.'

'Now, now,' said Captain. 'We're
quarrelling again.' And he called
out to Albertine.

While Peggoty and her little pigs,
including Pintsize, crawled into a
patch of nettles and lay still. Soon
all the animals were fast asleep . . .

except Pintsize who wasn't at all
sleepy.

So that's what they all did –
Captain in the darkest corner of his
stable,

Jigger under the
rhubarb leaves in
the vegetable patch,

Aunty Grace and Primrose side by
side under the great ash tree,

Egbert behind a pile of paper sacks in the barn so he could be near his lunch,

and Diana right in the middle of the sunniest field because she was very very silly!

Frederick went wherever his speckled hens did – and as they all went in different directions, he found that very difficult!

While Peggoty and her little pigs, including Pintsize, crawled into a patch of nettles and lay still. Soon all the animals were fast asleep . . .

except Pintsize who wasn't at all sleepy.

Chapter Three

Of all Peggoty's little pigs Pintsize was definitely the naughtiest. Say 'do this' and he'd do that. Say 'come here', and he'd go there. It was just the way he was. Some children are like that.

He waited until Peggoty was snoring,

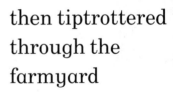

then tiptrottered through the farmyard

and down the lane

looking for really interesting things to do.

21

He hadn't gone far when he saw old Farmer Rafferty leaning on a gatepost and talking to the next-door farmer. Both of them were gazing up at the sky.

Cows are lying down. Sure sign of rain. It's coming, I can smell it.

Farmer Rafferty shook his head as he squinted at the sun.

he said,
and he laughed like a drain.

Pintsize pricked up his ears, (which isn't easy for a little pig).

And he jumped up and down in wild excitement.

I'm a pig.........
What's the matter with that little pig of yours?
Too much sun I expect.
How about a nice glass of lemonade?
Yes Please.
So that means
I can fly!.....
I can fly!.....
I can fly!.....
Yipeee!.........

Chapter Four

Flying was not nearly as easy as it looked. Pintsize stood up on his back trotters and flapped his front ones – trotters, he thought, would do just as well as wings.

But however hard he flapped (and flapping trotters is *not* easy) and however much he jumped up and down, he somehow never managed to take off. But Pintsize was not a giving-up sort of pig. He sat down and thought about it.

Nothing's ever easy at first. I mean, it took me days before I could walk. What was it Mama said to me? Practice makes perfect.

He was out in the meadow, practising his trotter flapping, when a crow spotted him and landed beside him.

What are you up to little piggy thing?

I'm learning to fly.

We've got a right one here!

The crow cackled and flew off to tell
his friends, then they all cawed
together until they got sore throats
– which served them right.

Suddenly Pintsize had an idea.

Upside and Down, they can fly. I've seen them. They'll teach me.

And he trottered off down to the muddy pond. 'Upside! Down!' he squealed, but they couldn't hear him, not with their heads in the mud.

In the end he got a long stick and poked
Upside in his down,

and Down somewhere else!

They were not at all pleased.

What do you want?

I want to fly.

'What, like this?' they quacked.
And they took off and looped a loop.

They dived

They looped the loop

swoop

Yes!
Yes!
Yes!

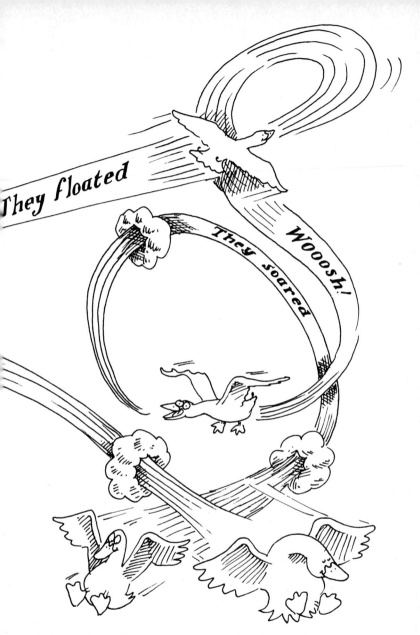

They floated

Wooosh!

They soared

They landed quite puffed. 'Like
that?' they quacked.

'Yes,' said Pintsize. 'Just like that. Please teach me. *Please*.' But they sniggered and snickered as ducks do.

'Just you watch me,' said Pintsize, and he climbed up the garden wall, took a deep breath and then ran . . .

until suddenly there was no more wall to run on . . . and he was flying through the air!

For one wonderful moment he was up there with the birds, but then something was pulling him down and down and down and he was turning over and over....

It's a pity Newton wasn't a Pig!

Then he landed,  in the muddy pond.

'Oh dear,' thought Albertine. 'I suppose I'd better do something about this.'

So she stood up and honked and
honked until all the animals woke
up and came running.

Pintsize was climbing the ladder
(and that's not easy if you're a pig)
up onto the haystack.

Peggoty closed her eyes, 'I'm not
looking,' she said.

We mustn't let him out of our
sight, otherwise he'll hurt
himself. Wherever he jumps
he's got to have a soft
landing. Quick Jigger,
you're the fastest.

Yap!
Yap
WWoo
Yap!

That's my Mum,
making the hard
decisions.

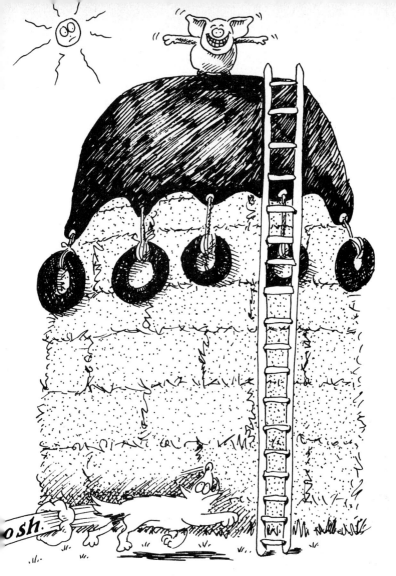

Jigger sprinted across the farmyard
until he was standing right under
the haystack. 'Don't jump!' he barked.
'Don't do it' . . . But Pintsize did it.

For one wonderful
moment he was
up there with the
birds, but then
something was
pulling him down
and down and
he was turning
over and over,
and then he landed –

SQUOOOOF!

on Jigger's back.

Jigger never knew
that little pigs
could be that heavy.
But he knew now.

And very soon they all knew,
because wherever Pintsize went
they had to go, so that whenever he
jumped, one of them was always
there for him to land on.

Every time he jumped he flew
further – or he thought he did, 'I can
fly,' he'd squeal. 'Pigs can fly.'

And it was true – well, sort of.

Pintsize flew as far as a pig ever had
flown, but then he'd drop like a
stone and knock all the air out of
poor Aunty Grace
(and that's
a lot of air),

or Primrose

or Captain

or Egbert

or Frederick.

But the one he liked landing on
most was Diana, because she was
very soft and very springy and very
spongy.

'Thanks, Diana,' he'd squeak and off he'd go again before anyone could catch him.

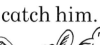

This can't go on.
You can say that again.
This can't go on.

I've tried everything I can, he just won't listen to me.

Something's got to be done.

Too true, quite right.

But what?

Everyone looked at Albertine to see if she'd had one of her ideas.
And of course she had.

'Don't you worry,' she said. 'I'll have a word with a friend of mine. I've got friends in high places you know. Just you keep your eye on Pintsize, all of you.'

Chapter Five

Drooping in the heat of the day, the animals did as Albertine said and trailed around the farm after Pintsize. They found him teaching his brothers and sisters. Standing up on his back trotters, Pintsize was explaining how a pig flies.

'You just wave these,' he said,
flapping his front trotters, 'and you
lift off. Simple when you know how.'

And all the little pigs stood up and
waved their front trotters.

While she wasn't looking, a buzzard
flew down and landed beside
Pintsize.

45

'Am I ready?' said Pintsize. 'Course I'm ready!' And before he knew it, the buzzard had picked him up and was soaring into the sky high above the farm.

'Nice view,' said the buzzard.

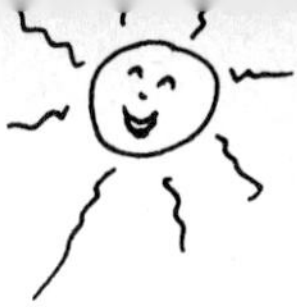

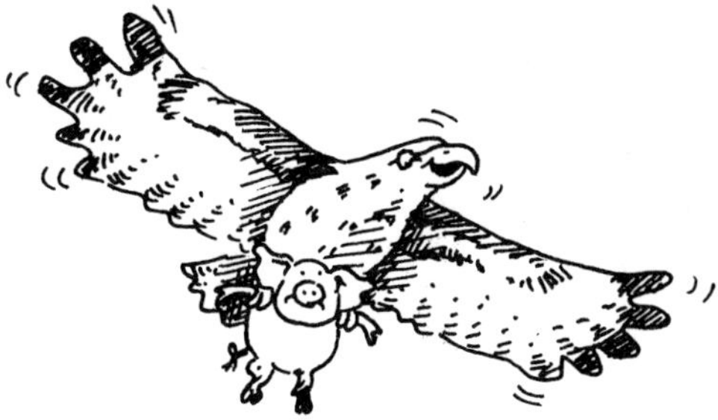

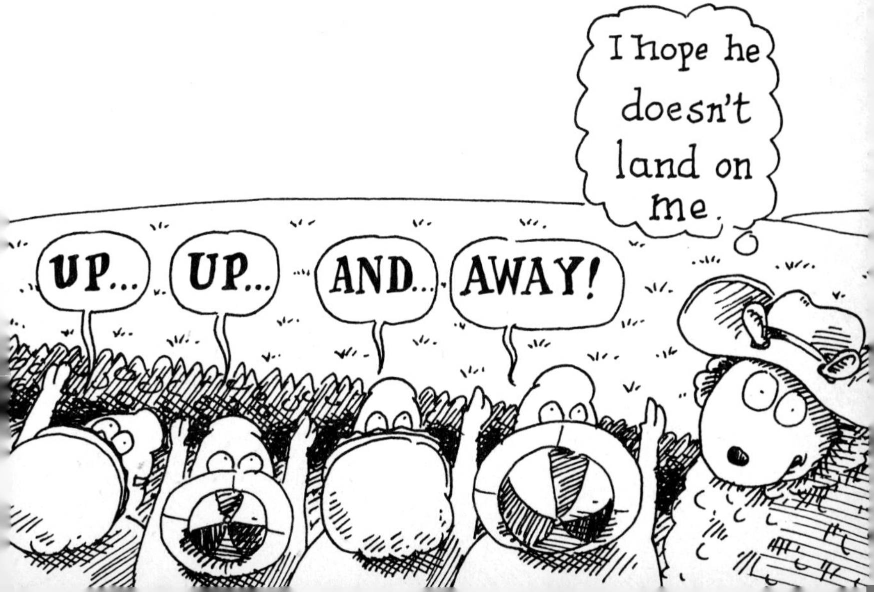

Pintsize looked down, and wished he hadn't. His stomach started to turn over and he began to feel very sick and very frightened. The animals below him were getting smaller

and smaller.

Then he couldn't see them any more.

49

'Take me down,' he squealed. 'Take me down.'

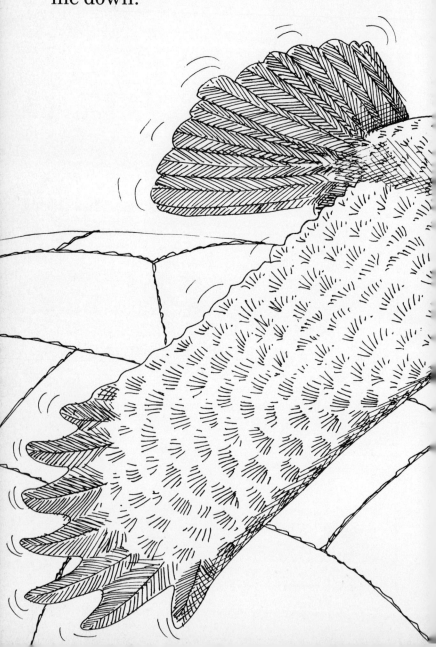

Pintsize tried to scream, but he couldn't. He was so frightened he couldn't even breathe . . .

51

The farm was coming closer and closer, it was getting bigger and bigger! He was going to crash!

Pintsize closed his eyes.

Putt
Putt
Putt
...ON ...ON
WHOOOOOOOOSH...
Please take me home... Please......
Like flying do you?
Pintsize has got the hang of it now.
Great idea Mum.
I know.

'Not yet,' said the buzzard, and as
they floated through the silent sky
they came to a cloud, a dark cloud.
'Don't like the look of that,' said the
buzzard a bit louder than he should.

Thunder rolled around the sky and the rain began to fall in great dollops.

'I want to go home,' squealed Pintsize. 'I want my mama.'

'All right,' said the buzzard, 'I'll drop you off.'

And he did just that!

Down below, Farmer Rafferty was talking to the next-door farmer again.

RAIN! I told you so, didn't I? It's raining cats and dogs.

'Yippee! Yarroo!' cried old Farmer Rafferty, and he did a sploshy rain-dance in a muddy puddle. But if he hadn't been so busy dancing, he'd have noticed that it wasn't raining cats and dogs at all – it was raining pigs. And one little pig in particular!

Pintsize tumbled through the air until at last he landed right in the middle of the....

DUNG HEAP

'Yes, Mama,' said Pintsize – and he
meant it. He snuggled into her and
buried his head in the dung so he
couldn't hear the thunder.

That evening Jigger saw Albertine as she was having her bath.

'Maybe,' said Albertine and smiled her goosey smile.

Meanwhile.......

On his tractor seat, Mossop
woke up.

61

Peggoty put her trotters over
Pintsize's ears so he couldn't hear
any more.

Oh for goodness sake, go back to sleep Mossop.

YAWNNN

'If you insist,' sulked Mossop and he
yawned hugely as cats do, closed his
one and single eye and slept.

The night came down, the moon came up and everyone slept on Mudpuddle farm.

Martians at Mudpuddle Farm

Chapter One

There was once a family of all
sorts of animals that lived in the
farmyard behind the tumble-down
barn on Mudpuddle Farm.

At first light every morning
Frederick, the flame-feathered
cockerel, lifted his eyes to the sun
and crowed and crowed until the
light came on in old Farmer
Rafferty's bedroom window.

One by one the animals crept out
into the dawn and stretched

and yawned

YAWNNNNNNNN

and scratched themselves.

But no one ever spoke a word – not
until after breakfast.

Early one morning old Farmer Rafferty looked out of his window. The corn was waving yellow in the sun. The stream ran clear and silver under the bridge, and the air was humming with summer.

The bees will be out flying today, and that means honey. And honey means money, and I need to buy a new tractor. The old one won't start in the mornings like it should. Get busy bees. Buzz my beauties, buzz!

Chapter Two

Deep in the beehive at the bottom
of the apple orchard, Little Bee was
getting ready for his first solo flight.

And off flew Little Bee out into the wide blue sky. Round and round he flew, looking for the clover field, but he couldn't find it anywhere.

So he buzzed down towards the old
tractor where Mossop, the cat with
the one and single eye, was trying
hard not to wake up.

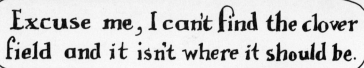

Mossop opened his eye.

Then he went back to sleep again.

The trouble was that Little Bee
didn't know his right from his left
or his left from his right.

Round and round he flew looking for the clover field, round and round till he began to feel giddy

Little Bee felt a great yawn coming on. He looked down for somewhere soft to sleep and then he saw the tractor with the old cat still asleep on the seat.

His tail looks nice and soft and warm. He won't mind, he won't even know I'm there.

And he was quite right about that.
Mossop never even felt Little Bee
land on his tail. He was too busy
dreaming. So Little Bee and Mossop
snoozed together in the sun and the
hours passed.

Chapter Three

Back in the beehive, Queen Bee
was getting worried. Little Bee had
been gone for hours now and
something had to be done.
She called all her bees together.

Right, forget pollen-gathering,
forget honey-making. Little
Bee is lost and we've got to
find him before dark else he'll
get cold and die. Follow me.

Ah-ha! Once more unto the breach!

Old Farmer Rafferty was milking
Aunty Grace, the dreamy-eyed
brown cow, when he heard the bees
coming. 'There they go,' he
chortled over his milk pail.

And then he began to sing as he
often did when he was happy.
He sang in a crusty, croaky kind of
a voice, and he made it up as he
went along.

Out in the clover field Diana the silly sheep

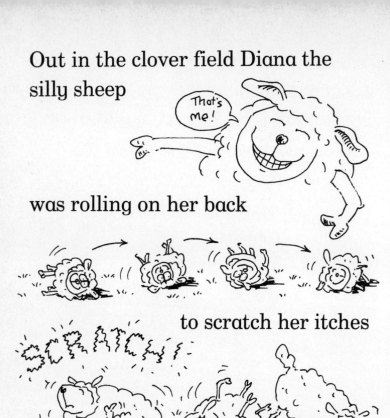

was rolling on her back

to scratch her itches

when she saw a great swarm of bees coming straight towards her.

She struggled to her feet and ran off towards the pond as fast as her legs could carry her. No one was at all surprised when she jumped right in. That's what she always did when there were bees about.

As usual it was Jigger, the almost always sensible sheep dog, who had to pull her out.

Silly sheep!

They can't sting you in the water. That's what my mother told me.

'And some mothers do have them,' thought Albertine from her island in the pond.

It's just bees buzzing. Nothing to worry about.

That's my Mum!

She's so calm in a crisis!

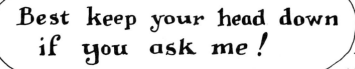

said
Upside
and Down.

So the two white ducks that no one could tell apart upside-downed themselves in the pond and stayed there all day long.

85

Captain, the great black carthorse who loved everyone and whom everyone loved, looked out over the clover field.

I don't like the look of this at all. There's too many of them and.... and they're coming this way!
Do pigs like honey, mummy?
I shouldn't be surprised if they do!

And sure enough, the sky above them suddenly darkened and the humming became a droning and the droning became a roaring.

The bees were right over their heads now and they sounded angry, very angry indeed!

DON'T MOVE!

But no one could move anyway. They were all too terrified, except Albertine of course.

'Albertine,' said Captain without moving his lips. 'What are we going to do?'

Chapter Four

Albertine thought her deep goosey thoughts for a moment. Then she said, 'Just follow me'. And she swam across the pond, waddled through the open gate and out into the cornfield beyond.

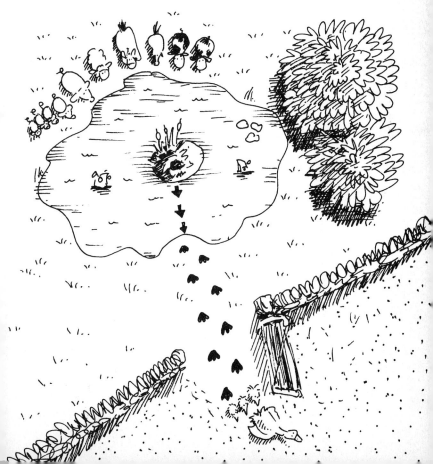

All the animals followed because
they knew that Albertine was the
most intelligent goose that ever
lived. If anyone knew what to do,
she would. They reached the middle
of the cornfield and looked up.
The bees were still following them.

Albertine began to run
round in a great big circle.

All the animals did the same, running round and round

And above them the bees all flew round and round and round

'I wish,' said Aunty Grace,

I wish someone would tell me why we're doing this. The bees aren't going away and I'm feeling giddy.

Me too dear!

said Primrose.

'Good,' said Albertine.

If you're feeling giddy, then the bees are feeling giddy.

She's so logical!

Not many people know this, but when a bee feels giddy, he gets sleepy too; and then he'll buzz off home to sleep. Never fails, you'll see. Keep going.

So round and round they all ran until suddenly the buzzing stopped. When they looked up the bees had all buzzed off, just as Albertine had said they would.

How do you do it?

It's called genius!

She's a wonderful mother too!

And so modest.

Chapter Five

The bees were flying home over the
farmyard when one of them
suddenly spotted Little Bee all
curled up asleep on Mossop's tail.
'Follow me,' said Queen Bee and down they flew.

Yes
Ma'am!

LITTLE BEE

'I got lost,' cried Little Bee.

'Soon,' Queen Bee yawned.
She could hardly keep her eyes
open, she was so sleepy.

And so that's what they all did.
Soon there was a great ball of
snoozing bees hanging on
Mossop's tail.

MEANWHILE....

Back in the cornfield, Captain had
a worried look on his face.
'Just look what we've done to
Farmer Rafferty's corn,' he said.
'Just look.' And they looked.

They had flattened out a huge circle in the corn. Not a single solitary stalk still stood standing.

They all heard him. He was
walking into the field singing his
♪ honey song.

Honey, oh honey, won't you b

When Farmer Rafferty reached
the middle of the cornfield, there
wasn't an animal to be found.
What he did find was a great
circle of flattened corn.

And he began to chortle and his
eyes began to twinkle.

Then off he went towards the farmhouse, counting on his fingers and muttering to himself.

He didn't know it, but from behind the farmyard wall the animals were watching and listening to every word.

'What's a Martian?' Diana asked and of course everyone looked at Albertine.

'Well,' she said, thinking very hard indeed, 'they walk stiffly like robots do and they carry ray-guns like Farmer Rafferty says.' The animals could hardly believe it, but if Albertine had told them then it had to be true. After all there was nothing Albertine didn't know.

Chapter Six

Farmer Rafferty was still counting
on his fingers when he passed by
the old tractor and noticed the ball
of bees hanging on Mossop's tail.

Oh dear me. My bees
have gone and swarmed.
Perhaps they couldn't find
the way back home. I'll
have to put them back in
their hive.

And he disappeared inside the
farmhouse.

While he was gone, the animals
crept back into the farmyard, just
in time to notice something coming
in through the farmyard gate.
It was dressed in white from
head to toe.

It wore a white helmet

and white gloves

and it walked stiffly like a robot,

and as it walked it puffed smoke
out of its ray-gun.

In its other hand it carried
a great big sack.

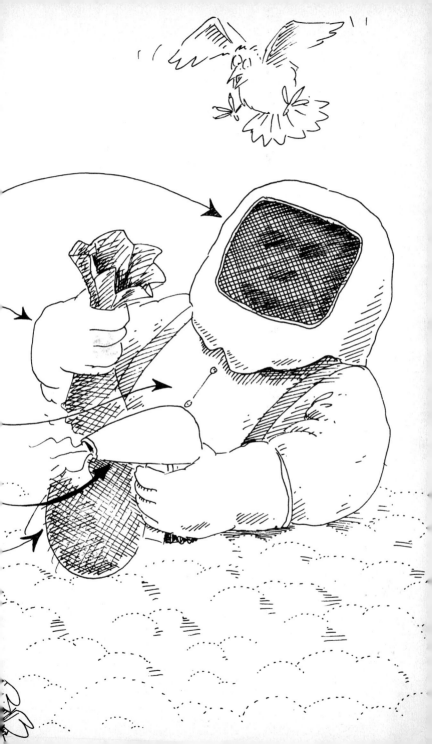

A Martian!

Diana cried. And she ran, they all ran. They ran until they came to the edge of the pond where they found Albertine washing herself.

'It's a Martian,' panted Jigger, the almost always sensible sheepdog.

Albertine smiled her goosey smile.

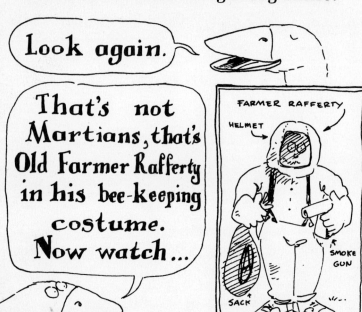

And they watched as old Farmer Rafferty puffed smoke around the swarm of bees.

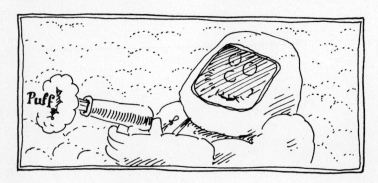

Farmer Rafferty scooped the bees into his sack, and off he went singing his honey song, with Queen Bee and Little Bee and all the others still snoozing inside.

Chapter Seven

Later that afternoon the first cars
arrived. Before long, Front Meadow
was filled hedge to hedge with cars,
and there were people everywhere.
Mossop, who had woken up by now,
walked down the lane and met
Jigger and the others.

CHILDREN'S CORNER ▼

TEAS ▶

Old Farmer Rafferty put up notices everywhere. I've eaten most of them.

KEEP OFF THE CORN!

▼ UP!

CUT FLOWERS

FRUIT ▶

DO NOT FEED THE ANIMALS!

VISITOR CENTRE ▼

TOM -A- TOES

Potatoes

117

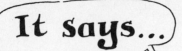

It says...

RAFFERTY'S CORN CIRCLE

GENUINE
MARTIAN CORN CIRCLE

To visit .... Two Pounds

Car Park .... Two Pounds

Martian Cream Tea ..... Two Pounds

(Honey <u>not</u> Strawberry Jam!)

'No one's going to believe a silly
story like that, are they?' said
Jigger; but when Albertine looked
at him he wished he hadn't said it.

'I think,' said Albertine 'that we
believe mostly what we want to
believe.'

Chapter Eight

That afternoon Farmer Rafferty
showed all the visitors round his
Martian corn circle.

After that they settled down on the
front lawn to a Martian cream tea.

He told them the story of the flying
saucer and the Martians that had
landed on Mudpuddle Farm, and
they swallowed it all (the cream
teas and the story) and went
home happy.

And old Farmer Rafferty was happy
too. He'd soon have enough money
to buy his new tractor.

All red and shiny it would be, with
a proper cab on it so he could
plough his fields without getting
wet and so Mossop could sleep out
of the wind.

But Mossop was quite happy out on
the old tractor in the farmyard.
None of the animals ever told him
about the day the bees swarmed on
his tail. They thought it might give
him bad dreams, and they didn't
want that.

The night came down, the moon came up, and everyone slept on Mudpuddle Farm.

Jigger's Day Off

Chapter One

There was once a family of all sorts of animals that lived in the farmyard behind the tumbledown barn down on Mudpuddle Farm.

Cocka-doodle-doooooo

At first light every morning, Frederick the flame-feathered cockerel lifted his eye to the sun and crowed and crowed . . .

until the light came on in old Farmer Rafferty's bedroom window.

One by one the animals crept out into the dawn and stretched and yawned and scratched themselves; but no one ever spoke a word, not until after breakfast.

You've got to get up, you've got to get up, you've got to get up in the morning!
That Frederick sure can play the HORN!

'Jigger my dear,' said old Farmer Rafferty, one hazy hot morning in September.

Corn's as high as a house. Fair weather ahead, they say. Time has come for harvest, Jigger. So I shan't be needing you all day. It's your day off my dear. Old Thunder sleeps in his shed all year - now it's his turn to do some work. Got to earn his keep, just like all of us. I'll just go and rub him down.

And off he went.

'One day off a year,' thought Jigger, the always sensible sheepdog. 'One day a year when I don't have to be sensible, when I can do what a dog likes to do.' And he licked his smiling lips, and wagged his dusty tail.

Old Thunder lived all by himself in a shed at the end of the yard. No one ever went near him because no one dared.

Pintsize had never seen Old
Thunder. He longed to peak in
through the crack in the doors.

can't
quite
see...

Mama,
let me look,
let me look

He squealed.

Peggoty warned him.

Don't you ever go near
Old Thunder, you hear me,
not ever.

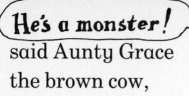 **He's a monster!**
said Aunty Grace
the brown cow,

 **I agree.**

and of course
Primrose agreed
with her as she
always did.

Matter of fact, most of the animals
thought Old Thunder was some sort
of monster.

So when old Farmer Rafferty opened the door of the shed that morning, all the animals went into hiding. Upside and Down turned upside down in terror. Mossop disappeared into a drainpipe. (Everyone was terrified of Old Thunder – except Egbert the greedy goat. He was always too hungry to be frightened.)

I wonder if OLD THUNDER collects up tasty rubbish?

Albertine the white goose gathered her goslings around her on her island in the pond and explained everything to them. She wasn't just an intelligent goose, she was a wise mother as well.

At that very and same moment, there was a roar from inside Old Thunder's shed, and he rumbled out into the yard belching smoke and dust. Old Farmer Rafferty sat high and happy on the driver's seat singing his heart out.

RUMBLE CRASH TTLE CLATTER

'See, children,' said Albertine gently. 'I told you that's all Old Thunder is, just an old combine harvester.'

Without him there'd be no straw to lie on in the winter and no corn to eat. Sometimes, children, I'm quite ashamed of my friends. I've told them and I've told them that Old Thunder only eats corn, but they just do not believe me.

One Man wer

Chapter Two

Old Thunder sailed majestically out
through the gate and into the corn
field beyond, his great cutters
turning like the wheels of a giant
paddle steamer. 'One man went to
mow, went to mow a meadow,' sang
old Farmer Rafferty in his crusty,
croaky kind of voice.

mow, went to mow a meadow,

went to mow a m

And behind him, Jigger, the
usually sensible sheepdog, slunk
through the gate and lay down in
the cut corn, his nose on the
ground in between
his paws.

SNIFF

He smelt something,

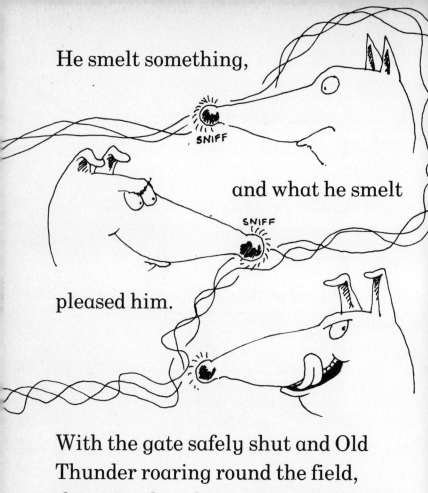

and what he smelt

pleased him.

With the gate safely shut and Old
Thunder roaring round the field,
the animals at last crept out of their
hiding places and stood watching by
the gate – all except Mossop who
had fallen asleep in his drain.

ZZZZZzz

'What's Jigger up to?' asked Diana the silly sheep, who always asked questions but never knew any answers.

Round and round the field went old
Thunder, churning out the straw
behind him in long and golden rows.
Round and round the field went
Jigger, slinking low to the ground.

And every now and then he would stop and stare at the square of standing corn, and every time he stopped, the square was a little bit smaller.

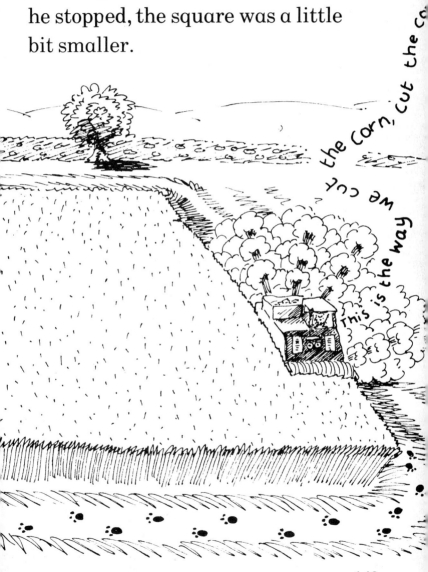

This is the way we cut the corn, cut the co

'We shouldn't be standing around in the sunshine,' said Captain.

Best go inside. those flies'll be at us soon.

So they did. Except for Egbert the goat who was busy chewing off the paint from the iron-barred gate.

150

At eleven o'clock Old Thunder

stopped,

shuddered,

coughed

and was silent. The birds sang
once more in the hedgerows.

Ever so carefully,
for he was stiff
in his knees,
old Farmer Rafferty
climbed down from
his seat and
sat down to rest
in the shade.

It was time for his morning milk.
He *always* had it at eleven o'clock
no matter where, no matter what.

What are you up to
Jigger my dear?

'I'm making sure old Thunder
doesn't miss anything,' said Jigger,
but he never took his eyes off the
standing corn.

And old Farmer Rafferty laughed
because he knew better.

Chapter Three

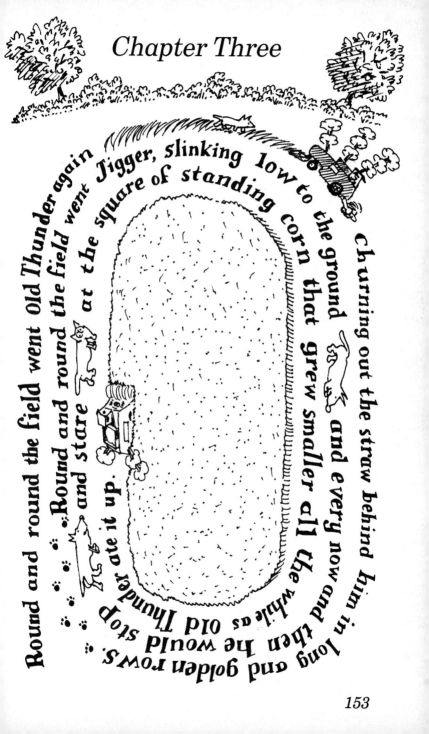

Round and round the field went old Thunder again

Round and round the field went Jigger, slinking low to the ground

churning out the straw behind him in

and stare at the square of standing corn that grew smaller all the while as old Thunder ate it up.

and every now and then he would stop

long and golden rows.

Albertine was passing the gate with her three yellow goslings peeping behind her. 'What's Jigger up to?' they peeped.

'Never you mind,' said Albertine, hurrying them on. 'Jigger's not himself today, he never is on his day off. This is the one day of the year he's not sensible, and I don't want you to watch.'

I think he's Jiggered.

'Only mad dogs go out in the mid-day sun,' grumbled Egbert the goat, who had finished eating the paint on the gate.

'Mad dogs and goats,' said Albertine, but quietly so that Egbert would not hear. She never liked to upset anyone.

155

At one o'clock old Thunder stopped again, shuddered, coughed and was silent. The birds sang once more in the hedgerows.

Ever so carefully, old Farmer Rafferty climbed down from his seat and sat down in the shade to eat his lunch – pasties and pickles.

He offered some to Jigger for he knew Jigger was partial to pasties. But Jigger was not interested in pasties – not today – he had his eye on the golden square of standing corn.

No thanks, can't stop for lunch.

Round and round the field went
Old Thunder again

churning out the straw behind him

in long and golden rows.

Round and round the field

went Jigger, slinking low

to the ground.

Captain plodded slowly down to the pond for a drink. 'Egbert,' he said, 'is Jigger still out there in this heat?'

'Must be mad, that dog,' said Egbert. 'Hasn't stopped all day. Round and round and round he goes – makes you dizzy just to look at him. Dunno why he bothers – he never catches anything.'

At four o'clock Old Thunder stopped again, shuddered, coughed and was silent. The birds sang once more in the hedgerows. Ever so carefully old Farmer Rafferty climbed down from his seat and walked off back towards the farmhouse to fetch his tea.

'Not much more to do,' he said as he went. 'Got 'em well and truly bottled up, have you, my dear? You'll never get 'em, Jigger, you never do.'

But Jigger was not listening to old Farmer Rafferty. He lay with his chin on his paws, his ears pricked forward towards the corn, his nose twitching.

Rabbits and hares, his nose told him,
rats and mice, moles and voles,
pheasants and partridges, beetles
and bugs.

He could hear them all rustling and bustling and squeaking and squealing in the little golden square of standing corn that was left.

Sooner or later he knew they would
have to make a run for it.

worry

Quake

Shivver

And he'd be waiting.

Chapter Four

Jigger my dear!

It was old Farmer
Rafferty calling
from the house and
whistling for him.

'Jigger! Come boy, come boy! I know
it's your day off, but the sheep have
broken out in Back Meadow.
Come boy, come boy!'

**I won't!
It's my one day off.
I'll be jiggered
if I'll go!**

'Jigger! Jigger!' Old Farmer Rafferty
was using his nasty, raspy voice.

You come here
Jigger, else there'll
be trouble.

If I go now I'll
have wasted my
whole day. There'll
be nothing left
in that corn for
me to chase
when I get back.

And then he had an idea.

WOOF!
BARK!

Jigger's barking brought all the
animals running,

waddling

and flying
to the gate.

'Bring 'em all out into the field,
Captain,' he called out. The animals
all looked at each other nervously.

Don't worry
Old Thunder's
fast asleep.
He's been
working hard.

And so they all went out into the field, all except Diana the silly sheep who refused to go anywhere near old Thunder, whether he was asleep or not. Jigger quickly explained everything to Captain. And he went off towards the farmhouse.

In no time at all, Captain had them all organised and ready.

Nothing must leave the standing corn. Jigger says that we're to chase it back if anything comes out.

169

So Peggoty and
her little pigs,

Including Pint size!

were sent to guard the north side of
the golden square of standing corn
along with Egbert.

I'd rather be
eating an old
shoe box

Primrose and Aunty Grace went off to guard the south side with Albertine and her goslings.

Captain himself stayed to guard the east side with Frederick the cockerel.

And Mossop,
the cat with
the one and
single eye
was sent off
to guard the
west side.

Wish it was
my day off
too!

Now you won't go to sleep will you?

Course not !
What makes you
think I'd do a
thing like that?

So on three sides of the golden square of standing corn the animals kept watch.

But for Mossop it was
all too much. The sun was hot

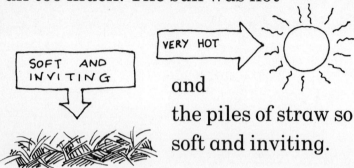

VERY HOT

SOFT AND
INVITING

and
the piles of straw so
soft and inviting.

He lay down,

closed his
one

and single
eye

and

quite forgot what he was there for.

Chapter Five

Mossop snored as he slept, and
inside the golden square of corn
they heard him and saw him
and took their chance.

One by one the little creatures of the cornfield left their hiding places. In one long line they left – westwards . . .

Tee hee!

Rabbits first, then mice and

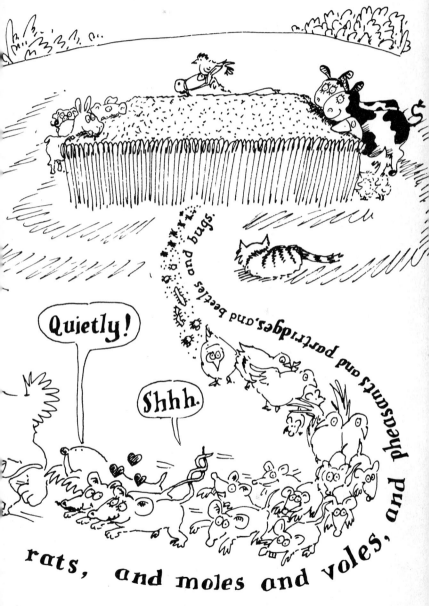

They tiptoed past the snoring cat
and out across the open field until
they reached the safety of the
hedgerow, where they vanished.

Chapter Six

Not long after this Jigger came haring back through the gate.

Didn't let anything escape, did you?

Not a one. Proper job we did for you Jigger, proper job.

And all the animals hurried back to the farmyard just in case Old Thunder woke up again – all of them except Mossop who still lay fast asleep in a pile of straw.

'Just this last little square to finish,
Jigger,' said old Farmer Rafferty
after he had finished his tea. 'Be
finished by sundown, in spite of
those darned sheep.'

But Jigger was not listening. He had other things on his mind. As Old Thunder started up again he was ready and waiting for the first of the little creatures to break out of their hiding place.

Round and round the field went Old Thunder for the last time, slinking low to the ground. Round and round the field went Jigger for the last time, slinking low to the ground.

and round the Field

time churning out straw behind him in long and golden rows. Round

By the time the sun set behind the tumble-down barn, not a stalk of corn was left standing. And nothing had come out, no rabbit, no rat, no mouse, no vole, no mole, no pheasant, no partridge, no beetle and no bug.

Nothing.

'Well I'll be jiggered,' said Jigger.

I don't believe it!

I just don't believe it!

I could have sworn there were hundreds of them in that corn. I could smell 'em. I could hear 'em.

'It's the sun, Jigger,' said Mossop, who had just woken up. 'Does strange things to you.'

I can tell you Jigger nothing came past me when I was on guard. We'll they wouldn't dare, would they?

And he yawned hugely as cats do.

Jigger looked at Mossop sideways and wondered.

'Had a good day off, Jigger my dear?' old Farmer Rafferty shouted as he passed by high up on Old Thunder.

And old Farmer Rafferty laughed
and laughed, until the laughter
turned into a song once again.

ne man and his dog, (woof! woof!) went to mo
It's been a long day. Don't know about you, Jigger, but I'm just about ready for bed.
Tee hee!

And the night came down and the moon came up and everyone slept on Mudpuddle Farm.